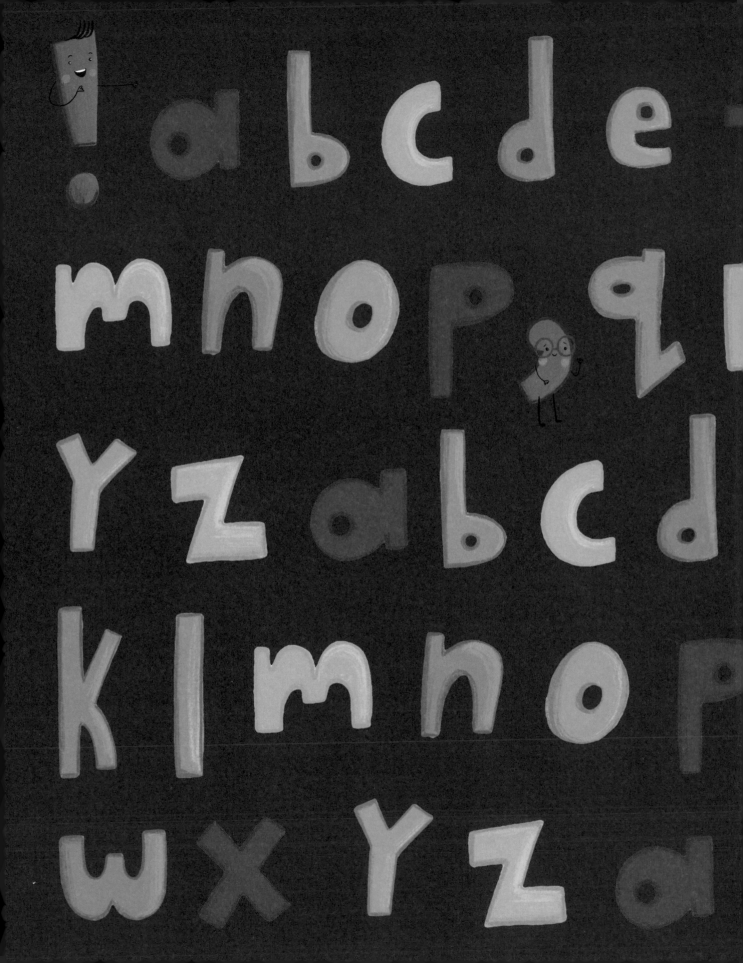

The DAY PUNCTUATION Came to TOWN

To all the teachers,
librarians, and booksellers
who encourage and inspire
children every day!
—K. G.

To Mom and Dad.
—S. S.

Published by Familius LLC, www.familius.com

Familius books are available at special discounts for bulk purchases, whether for sales
promotions or for family or corporate use. For more information, contact Familius Sales at
559-876-2170 or email orders@familius.com.

Library of Congress Cataloging-in-Publication Data
2019936502

Print ISBN 9781641701457
Ebook ISBN 9781641702065

Printed in China

Edited by Brooke Jorden and Kaylee Mason
Cover and book design by David Miles and Derek George

10 9 8 7 6 5 4 3 2 1

First Edition

The DAY PUNCTUATION Came to TOWN

KIMBERLEE GARD

illustrations by

SANDIE SONKE

FAMILIUS

A new family moved to Alphabet City—the Punctuations.

Exclamation Point led the way to their first day at a new school. "Let's hurry!" he exclaimed. "I can't wait to get there! We are going to have so much fun!" Exclamation Point was always excited about something.

Question Mark wondered what it would be like. "Do you think everyone will be nice? Are we going the right way? Should we ask for directions?"

Period followed, bringing the line to a close. "Let's go. I'll tell you when to stop."

Comma kept pausing. "Wait for me, please."

When they walked into school, Exclamation Point burst forward. "Hi, everyone!" The little letters stared. "Who are you?" they asked. "You don't look like letters." "We're not letters!" Exclamation Point explained. "We're the Punctuation family!" "The Punctuation *who*?" The letters were confused.

"I'm Exclamation Point, and this is Question Mark,
Comma, and Period.

We're different from letters, but we love being around words!"

The Punctuations joined the class. The letters worked to make words. Exclamation Point, Question Mark, and Period joined in the fun.

Exclamation Point added excitement to words. Question Mark asked a lot of questions.

Period brought each sentence to a tidy end.

Comma tried not to get stepped on and fit in wherever he could

As the day wore on, Comma began to feel smaller and smaller.

"The letters love making words, but I just get in the way and keep them apart," he whispered to himself. "No one wants me here."

When no one was looking, Comma snuck out the door.

Inside the classroom, Exclamation Point was creating
a great deal of excitement. The letters were cheering and
hurrying to make words.

"Shouldn't we quiet down?" Question Mark asked, but no one heard her over the noise. The letters kept making words, faster and *faster* and *FASTER!*

Soon words were everywhere. There were so
many words, they all became jumbled. Period hurried
to stop them, but the letters tripped over her and
collided. With a thundering crash, the letters fell, one
after another, until they all tumbled through the door,
spilling into the hall.

Comma stared in shock. The letters were piled, the words all tangled.

Exclamation Point, Question Mark, and Period ran into the hallway. They saw the heap of letters, and then they saw Comma.

"What are you doing out here?" Question Mark asked.

"I didn't think anyone wanted me around," Comma sighed. "I just slow everything down."

"Comma, without you, things become a disaster!" Exclamation Point said, pointing to the pile of letters and words.

Period nodded. "Slowing things down is your job, and words need you."

"Didn't you know? When we're with words, we all have a job to do?" Question Mark asked.

"I add excitement!" Exclamation Point burst out.

"Have a question?" Question Mark asked. "That's what I'm here for."

"And I put a stop to things," Period said.

"We're the Punctuation family, and we all work together to help letters and the words they make."

The Punctuations helped the letters back into the classroom.

When the letters began making words again,
Comma stood right in the middle.

The letters looked confused. "What are you doing?"
  "It's my job," Comma said. "From now on, I'll help keep things in order."
  "How?" the letters asked.

It was Comma's turn to explain. "We all work together.
Words need punctuation, and punctuation needs words."

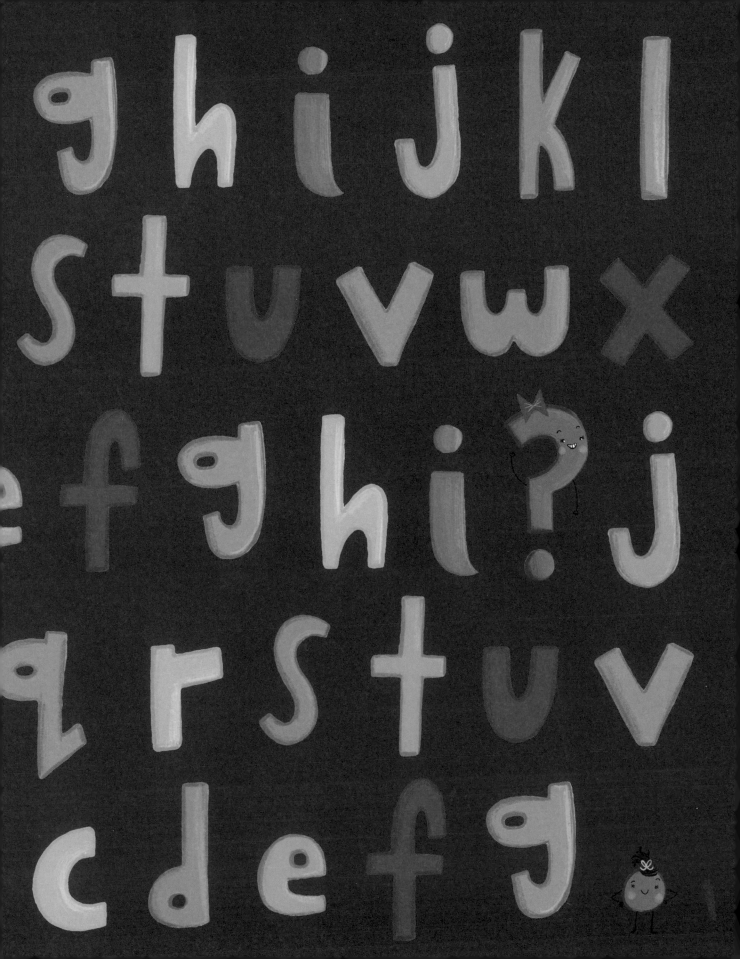